To Jude,

Write down all
of your ideas!

Dan Martin -

Written by
Darren Sardelli

Illustrated by
Max Hergenrother

For Mason and Aidan, Grant and Kole—
Your possibilities are as vast as your imagination.
Dream big and do what makes you happy!

Published by Laugh-A-Lot Books, New York

ISBN # 978-0-578-64853-8
LCCN #2020936280

Publisher's Cataloging-in-Publication Data

Names: Sardelli, Darren, author. | Hergenrother, Max, illustrator.

Title: What if? / written by Darren Sardelli ; illustrated by Max Hergenrother.

Description: Great Neck, NY: Laugh-A-Lot Books, 2020. | Summary: Imagine a world where pencils open portals, pictures paint people, and basketballs are square. Imagination takes flight in this crazy, wacky, mixed-up book of questions.

Identifiers: LCCN: 2020936280 | ISBN: 978-0-578-64853-8

Subjects: LCSH Children's poetry, American. | Humorous poetry, American. | Humorous poetry. | BISAC | POETRY / Juvenile Fiction | JUVENILE FICTION / Stories in Verse | JUVENILE FICTION / Humorous Stories | JUVENILE FICTION / Imagination & Play

Classification: LCC PZ8.3 .S234 2020 | DDC 811/.5/4--dc23

Manufactured in China.
10 9 8 7 6 5 4 3 2 1 20 21 22 23 24 25 26 27 28 29 30

LAUGH-A-LOT BOOKS encourages imagination, creativity, and fun.
Write down your ideas, set goals for yourself, chase your dreams,
and never give up. You are capable of extraordinary things.
If you believe you can do something, you'll find a way.
We wish you all the success in the world!

Please visit us online at
www.laughalotbooks.com

LAUGH-A-LOT BOOKS
New York

WHAT IF

What if Bigfoot brought you breakfast?
What if garden gnomes were real?

What if Cupid made each chipmunk fall in love with every seal?

HOME

What if witches lived in closets
and a dragon warmed your tea?

What a crazy, wacky, mixed-up place
this world would surely be!

What if pictures painted people?
What if mountains moved on maps?
What if lightning tried to kiss you?
What if doughnut holes were traps?

What if baths were built with beehives?
What if toilets charged a fee?
What a crazy, wacky, mixed-up place
this world would surely be!

ICKLES

What if pickles gave you powers?
What if ice cream were a fruit?
What if chairs and couches shocked you?
What if every bug were cute?

What if tortoises could teleport
and grizzly bears could ski?
What a crazy, wacky, mixed-up place
this world would surely be!

What if artichokes got angry?
What if ceiling fans could cry?
What if bouncy balls and bean bags
fell directly from the sky?

324

What if tie-dye were a number?
What if two came after three?
What a crazy, wacky, mixed-up place
this world would surely be!

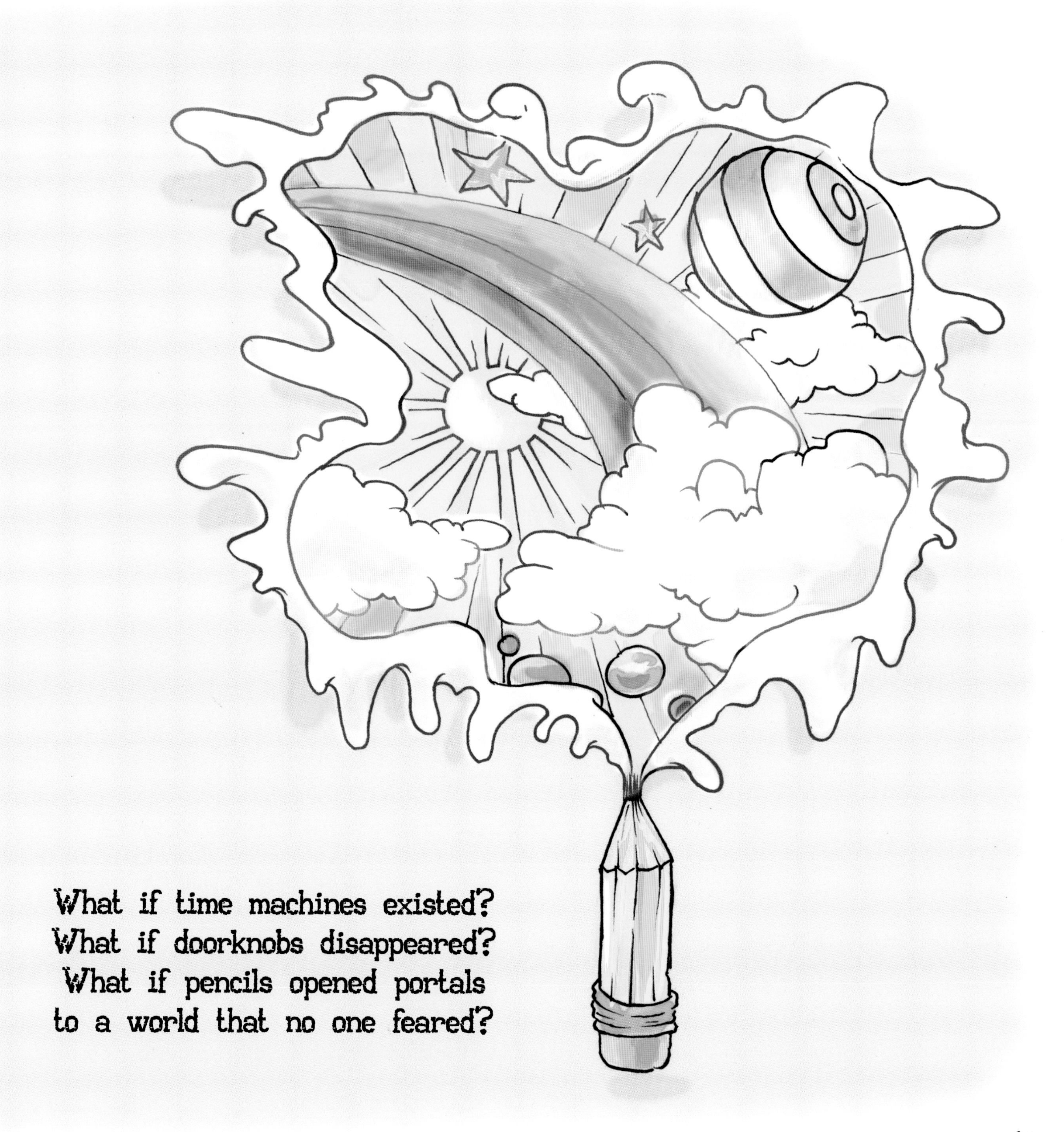

What if time machines existed?
What if doorknobs disappeared?
What if pencils opened portals
to a world that no one feared?

What if kids had magic carpets?
What if rocket ships were free?
What a crazy, wacky, mixed-up place
this world would surely be!

MASON
8

What if wheels were sharp and pointy?
What if basketballs were square?
What if microscopic monkeys
built their houses on your hair?

What if genies lived in lava lamps
and monsters roamed the sea?
What a crazy, wacky, mixed-up place
this world would surely be!

What if rubber bands were rock stars? What if soccer balls could kick?

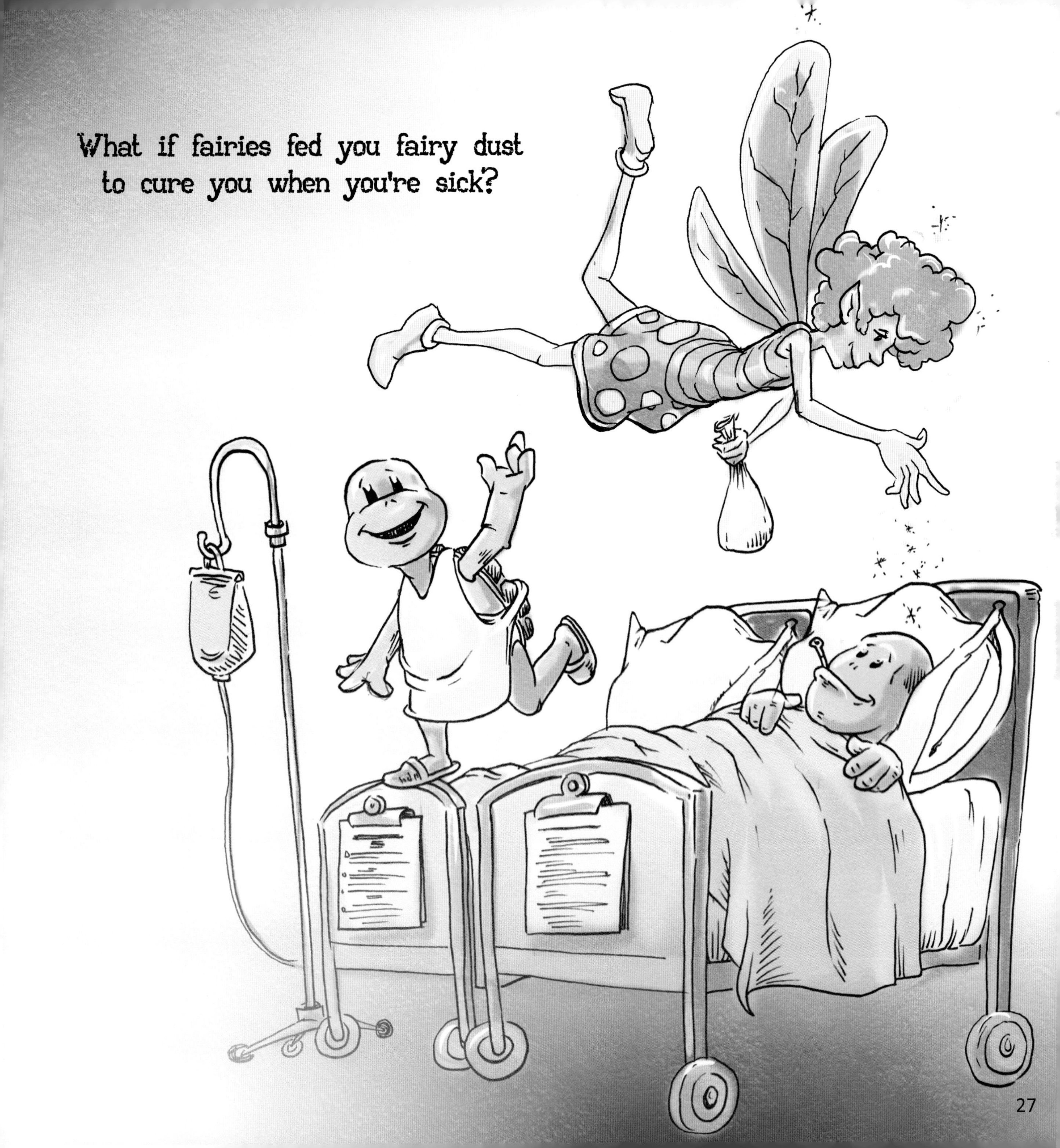
What if fairies fed you fairy dust
to cure you when you're sick?

GRANT
+
KOLE

What if golden coins were hidden
in a branch on every tree?
What a crazy, wacky, mixed-up place
this world would surely be!

USM
Roses are red.
Violets are grand.
Dirt is OK,
but nothing beats sand!

What if gum grew on the sidewalk?
What if grains of sand could talk?
What if spider webs were hammocks
and your hands were colored chalk?

What if raindrops melted rainbows?
What if people thought like me?
What a crazy, wacky, mixed-up place
this world would surely be!

THE END!
KH